Anton
can do
magic

THE GREAT
SORCAR
WORLD'S GREATEST MAGICIAN

Ole Könnecke

GECKO PRESS

First American edition published in 2011 by Gecko Press USA, an imprint of Gecko Press Ltd.

A catalog record for this book is available from the US Library of Congress.

Distributed in the United States and Canada by
Lerner Publishing Group, Inc.
241 First Avenue North
Minneapolis, MN 55401 USA
www.lernerbooks.com

This translation first published in 2010 by Gecko Press
PO Box 9335, Marion Square, Wellington 6141, New Zealand
info@geckopress.com

English language edition © Gecko Press Ltd 2010

Original title: Anton kann zaubern
© Carl Hanser Verlag München Wien 2006
Text and illustrations © Ole Könnecke

Translator: Catherine Chidgey
Editor: Penelope Todd
Typesetting: Luke Kelly, New Zealand
Printing: Everbest, China

ISBN hardback: 978-1-877467-37-0

For more curiously good books, visit **www.geckopress.com**

Here comes Anton.
Anton has a magic hat.
A real one.

Anton wants to do some magic.
He wants to make something disappear.

A tree.

Anton stares at the tree.

Then he does some magic.

That's funny—the tree is still there.

That tree is probably too big.

There's a bird. That's smaller.

Anton does some magic.

The bird is gone.

Anton can do magic!

Here comes Luke.

"I can do magic!" shouts Anton.

"You can't," says Luke.
"I can," says Anton.

"Can't," says Luke.
"I'll make you disappear!" says Anton.

Anton does some magic.

Luke is gone.

Anton has made Luke disappear!

But Luke shouldn't disappear.

Anton wants to bring Luke back.

That's not Luke.
Or is it?

"Is that you, Luke?"

Luke must not fly away.

Here come the girls.

And Luke!

Greta's bird is gone.
Nina is helping her look for it.
So is Luke.

"I'll make the bird come back," says Anton.
"Ha ha," says Luke.

Anton does some magic.

The bird is back!

Anton can do magic.